T

MW00439794

The Santa Fe Trilogy III—
GOING BACK HOME

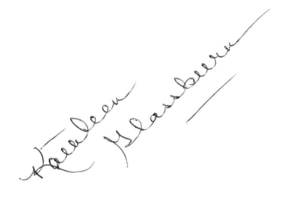

Kathleen Glassburn

To Richard—
For all your love and support.

And—
In Memory of James Garner

The Santa Fe Trilogy III
GOING BACK HOME

Janice McKenna, third contestant in the Barrel Race for Women over Eighteen, took a deep breath. Slowly exhaling, she stared down the chute and sized up the cloverleaf-designed course.

Rory stood with his ears erect, body tense, eager to move.

Gripping her legs against his sides and loosening the reins, she shouted, "Go!"

An electric monitor flashed as Janice and Rory crossed a red line and bolted into the ring, moving toward the first of three fifty-five-gallon metal barrels. They looped it smoothly to the right in a perfect teardrop shape.

Charging toward the second barrel, they formed another teardrop to the left.

Heading toward the last barrel, they swerved, cutting it a little wide, but Rory picked up speed and recovered lost time.

Janice grabbed the pommel, lifted herself out of the saddle, and pressed him on.

A light flashed as they crossed the red line and flew back through the chute.

Sinking into her saddle, Janice gave a long, soft "Whoa."

When Rory came to a complete stop, she patted his shoulders, first one then the other. "Good boy...Good boy," she chanted and rubbed his withers.

The announcer's voice bellowed over a loud speaker. "17.08 seconds for Janice McKenna on Rory. Hard time to beat."

Two earlier entries had come in at .40 and .42 seconds longer. Five more to go.

Thirty minutes later it was over, and the announcer boomed, "Our grand prize goes to Janice McKenna on Rory. Give them a big hand, folks."

Janice and Rory walked to the ring's center.

One judge attached a blue ribbon to Rory's bridle.

Another judge handed a $1,000 check to Janice.

She and Rory did a final jog around the ring, accompanied by the crowd's loud clapping.

As she dismounted in the warm-up area, several riders approached to congratulate her and pat Rory.

He drank from a communal water trough before Janice walked him to the parking area. She tied him to the trailer and gave him a brisk rubdown, along with a couple of molasses horsey cookies. Next, she hooked him inside and headed back to the ring, looking for Luke and Snake.

The two of them were at the end of the front row, Snake on the bench, Luke beside him in his wheelchair. A bulldogging event had started.

"You did great," Snake said when Janice sat down next to him. "Only been back in the saddle a couple of years. Taking the top prize is impressive."

"Mighty fine," Luke rasped.

"I'm going to use the money for repairs on paddocks. Can't get Rory to stop cribbing and those fences are showing it." She smiled. "That's his only bad habit."

Angie, Luke's former employee, walked by conversing with Fred Palmer. He hulked over Angie by a good foot. As expected, Palmer, who owned a small place with a few horses two miles from Cerrillos Ranch, had taken top honors in the roping events.

What's she doing with him? Janice wondered.

Even though they seemed to be talking seriously, Angie glanced at her.

"Congrats!" She tipped her red baseball hat.

"You got firm control of that gelding," Fred said. "Howdy Snake. Howdy Luke."

Angie ignored both Snake and Luke.

"Howdy Fred," Snake, ever the gentleman, made eye contact.

"Hmppf," Luke snorted and never looked up.

Janice knew he didn't think much of Palmer—something about a purchase offer—and he disliked Angie because of her careless ways. Leaning toward him, Janice said, "Are you ready to go? Had enough?"

"My rocker would be good."

Janice released the brakes on Luke's wheelchair and began to haltingly roll him away.

Snake took the handles. "Let me do that." He easily maneuvered Luke and his chair through the crowd, out of the arena, and along the path that led to their truck and trailer.

***

Luke never attended another rodeo, and he never spent much time in his rocking chair either. A few days after Janice's win, Snake brought a rented hospital bed for him, and set it up in front of the television. Janice used her long-abandoned nursing skills over the coming few weeks, making Luke as comfortable as possible. According to his wishes, he died in that bed, in the front room of the bunkhouse, with Janice holding one hand, Snake holding the other.

Luke's last words were, "Mary Lou...up there...beckoning."

Also, according to his wishes, they had him cremated and spread his ashes with no religious service or fanfare, merely a few words said by each of them, atop the mesa that overlooked his ranch.

Snake said, "Thanks for your trust. I'll help take care of things."

Janice said, "Thanks for taking me in. You gave my life a new purpose."

The ashes of Luke's daughter, Mary Lou, had been spread on that same mesa some thirty years before.

***

In this, Janice's second autumn at Cerrillos, she felt overwhelmed by the responsibilities after Luke died. Even though extremely sick, he had kept his mental faculties. She was able to consult him about all matters relating to the ranch and the horses.

Now, she often said to Snake, "Thank goodness you moved out here. I don't think I could do this on my own."

"Glad to pitch in. Frankly, sleeping on one of the bunks is better than that cramped apartment in town."

"It's reassuring to know you're here at night...in case something happens to a horse." She shook her head. "My trip to Seattle is coming up soon."

"Have you contacted Angie? To see if she can spend some time at this place each day?"

"I did. A few months ago. Before Luke...He didn't want that woman coming around, but I coaxed him, saying she was good with the mechanical stuff I can't do. He finally relented."

"Why hasn't she come out?"

"She's working at Palmer's." Janice hesitated. "Besides, she doesn't want to be anywhere near you."

"I thought that was over a long time ago."

"Mind if I ask what that is?"

"Not fair of me to say. If you ever get Angie alone, ask for her version."

"Sorry to be nosey."

"You're fine. It's not up to me to talk about her business."

For about the tenth time, Janice questioned negative remarks Angie had made regarding Snake on that first frightening trail ride. She accused him of possessiveness and perhaps even violence. She told Janice about leaving her husband in Pittsburgh and coming to Santa Fe with Snake. Was any of it true?

A remark Luke once made came to mind: "That woman has a powerful imagination."

When she led Janice on the ride, Angie would have assumed she'd never see her again. She could have fabricated anything. Unexpectedly, Janice landed at

Cerrillos Ranch with Angie's job, and as soon as she got to know him, Snake's courtesy and kindness impressed her. An obvious discrepancy existed. It was just as well that Angie refused the job Janice offered her. If forced to take sides, she would definitely be with Snake.

Soon after she'd approached Angie, the boys who had been involved in a mine shaft accident the previous winter—Mike and Andy and Pete—came to the ranch looking for tasks to do. She hired them on the spot. Surprisingly, they accomplished a lot. After school they did feeding, watering, and stall cleaning. Plus, they were good company. Adam and Jesse, Janice's grown sons, had been a lot like these boys at twelve. Always eager and polite and sometimes too adventurous. Maybe helping with the mine accident made her special to the local boys. Maybe they wanted extra money. Maybe they needed someplace to hang out. Mike and Andy came from difficult home situations with single mothers who were seldom in evidence. Pete had a hard time making friends. After the accident, Mike and Andy started to include Pete in their ramblings.

"We stay away from abandoned mines," Mike reassured Janice.

Snake had finished a construction project, and said he'd be happy to work full time at the ranch. In addition, he was good company, too. Having him around eased the loss of Luke. Janice had become attached to the old guy, almost like a father. Her husband, Rod, died two years before. Her sons, while affectionate, didn't have much need of a mother these days. Her parents were long gone. And, her younger brother was far away in the Navy. Too many losses. Mike and Andy and Pete filled the void, along with Snake.

**

One morning, shortly before Janice left for Seattle, Fred Palmer stopped by Cerrillos. She was talking to the boys out by the paddocks. They had worked alongside Snake doing the fence mending, and she was giving them an early Christmas bonus.

"I want to talk to you," Fred barged in.

"Sure. I'm almost finished here." Janice turned back to Mike. "I appreciate all your work. You guys have done a great job." She handed each one an envelope with a card and a crisp twenty dollar bill inside.

Andy and Pete turned red and looked down at their hands, but Mike said, "Thanks! We like it here." The others nodded.

She turned toward Palmer. "What can I do for you, Fred?"

"I got something for you. My mare's too old for competing. You could use her for trail rides. Dusty's a good girl. Not touchy at all."

"That sounds interesting." Janice was eager to learn more about the horse business as well as the neighbors. "I'd like to come by and check her out."

"Sure. Sooner rather than later. I need to find a job for her. Can't keep up with the training and feeding."

"We'll drive over after dinner."

"You and Snake?"

"Yes. Is it okay if I bring him?" Why should he care?

Palmer chewed pensively on his tobacco. "That'll be fine."

A few hours later, Janice and Snake made the short drive in his black pickup. Along the way, they talked about the advisability of adding another horse.

"Expensive to keep her," Snake didn't know about Janice's financial situation as the widow of a cardiologist.

"I'm down one since Murphy and need another dependable mount." The breeze blew her hair into Janice's eyes. She flicked reddish-brown strands away. "I don't like to use Rory on trail rides, and Dusty sounds like she'd be safe."

"Maybe you're right."

There'd been no accidents at the ranch since Murphy threw Angie, injuring her spine. This horrific incident had resulted in Janice being hired.

As Murphy aged, he had become erratic. Angie's fall was the first of several less severe misbehaviors. They had put him down after he ran over Janice while she led him out to the paddocks. Fortunately, nothing broke, but she was bruised-up plenty.

"He's too unpredictable," Snake had said. "You can't be around a dangerous animal that size." He put an arm over Janice's slumped shoulders. "It's hard, but part of the deal. Murphy's not a headstrong terrier."

She had reluctantly agreed. This was the first horse loss she'd been forced to contend with since taking over the ranch.

After Janice and Snake checked out Dusty, they decided she'd be a welcome addition. Buckskin and just a bit smaller than Rory at fifteen hands, she approached them for carrots and pats without hesitation. Then, she willingly stepped into the trailer, got hooked up, and rode quietly to Cerrillos where Janice led her around before putting her in Murphy's old stall next to Rory.

Within days, Rory and Dusty became best buddies, whinnying to each other if they were separated, romping and playing together in their shared paddock at turn-out. Rory even quit cribbing so much.

Janice began to refer to Dusty as his "girlfriend."

***

After she left for Seattle, as promised, Janice got a call from Snake every day. Most of the time, things at the ranch were the same, but hearing his deep voice always gave her a tug of yearning for the place. During one conversation, he did say, "I ordered hay from a new supplier."

"Whatever you think," Janice said, completely trusting his judgment.

This traditional Thanksgiving with Ilsa went well. Baron and Scamper, the dog and cat Janice had left with her neighbor, were friendly but stayed by Ilsa's side. Both boys seemed happy to see Janice. But they had new girlfriends and were eager to return to Bellingham.

Next year maybe they'll all be here, she hoped.

Neither Adam nor Jesse had dated much in high school, merely attending proms and that sort of thing. They had hung out with a group of kids, boys and girls alike, but no special girls.

Sure different from me.

Janice had dated the same guy until she left for the University of Washington in Seattle. Bobby attended Washington State in Pullman, three hundred miles away, with the goal of becoming a veterinarian. She went to nursing school, met Rod McKenna who was in medical school, and they married around the time she started work at Northwest Hospital. Since she hadn't ever gone back to Montana, Janice never heard anything about Bobby after their break-up. When thinking of him, which was seldom, she assumed he was there, taking care of horses and other livestock. Since Adam and Jesse were so involved with their girls during this current visit, spending hours texting back and forth, she began to recall her own first love with wistfulness.

Right after Thanksgiving, on his call, Snake said, "For the last day or so, Rory hasn't been eating much."

"He usually gobbles up his grain and takes his time with the hay," she said.

"I'm wondering if it's that new hay."

"Maybe. How are the other horses?"

"They seem fine." He hesitated. "I'll be extra watchful of him."

About this time, during a walk around Seattle's Green Lake, DeeDee Bradley, Janice's best friend, said, "Do you think you're ready to see Jeff Crandall? He's still single." This was the divorced doctor Janice had refused to meet the year before.

"Sounds like fun," she immediately said.

DeeDee went into overdrive, and soon began organizing a dinner party for eight. There would be Jeff and Janice, two other familiar couples, Don and DeeDee.

Janice was astonished at the availability of everyone with such short notice during the Holidays.

"They want to hear about your new life," DeeDee said.

Wearing a casual red sweater and black wool slacks, Janice arrived at the Bradley house, which was full of wonderful cooking smells, early in order to help out. Jeff Crandall was already there. He had an easy, direct smile and engaging blue eyes that met hers straight on.

"It's nice to finally meet," he said, extending a hand. "DeeDee's spoken of you often." His low, soothing voice, kind of like Snake's, put her at ease.

"It is good to meet." She hasn't told me that much about you. This did seem strange. DeeDee wasn't known for keeping quiet.

"You're working on a ranch in New Mexico?"

"Actually, more than working. I own it."

Jeff's eyes widened. "Quite a responsibility."

"It is that."

Janice explained Luke's legacy. "He expected me to take excellent care of the fifteen horses, as he'd always done."

"You grew up on a ranch, right?"

17

"In Montana."

"So you have experience. How did you get away now?"

"I have good help. A man from the area and three boys are there. They keep the place in tip-top shape, and I get a daily update call from Snake."

"Snake?"

"It's a strange nickname, I know." Janice grimaced. "He's quite tall and thin. I'm phobic about snakes, but he's a great guy."

After some talk about the Holidays, Jeff said, "How long are you staying in Seattle?"

"I'm here until after DeeDee's New Year's Eve party. I missed it last year."

"I'll be there." His smile seemed to say, Glad you will be, too.

"Sounds good. I need to go help with dinner. We can talk more later, if you want."

As she walked to the kitchen, Janice felt his eyes on her. She turned at the swinging door. Jeff lifted his glass of red wine, and then ambled into the family room where Don Bradley sat humming along with favorite carols. He was a sentimental cardiologist who had been a partner of her husband's. Rod used to love Holiday music, too.

The weekend after Thanksgiving, DeeDee always put up her enormous tree, lavishly decorated the house, and started playing Christmas music.

"You're getting along well," she said when Janice joined her at the sink.

"He seems like a really good guy."

"Told you."

"How come you didn't tell me more about him?"

"Oh...well...I don't really know that much."

There was a clatter as DeeDee dropped a pan while pulling it out from an organized, divided cupboard. Janice turned her attention to the remodeled kitchen. "Nice refrigerator," she said. It was enormous.

"A Sub-Zero." DeeDee beamed.

Not knowing what this meant, and not feeling like an explanation, Janice said, "What can I do?"

"Here," DeeDee handed her a peeler and a large kettle. "You can get these potatoes ready to boil."

She served huge shrimp and crudites for appetizers, medium rare London Broil with garlic mashed potatoes and several vegetable dishes. For dessert, there was a tray with bells painted on it mounded with frosted and sprinkled cookies.

She's baked already.

Janice enjoyed seeing the old friends from her couple days with Rod more than she expected. They slipped right into congenial talk about the Holidays, children, and life on her ranch. It felt like she was an out-of-towner being entertained while visiting.
Crystal on the beautifully-set table sparkled from a dimly-lit chandelier and candles. The mood became nostalgic with an aged Cabernet and more Holiday music playing softly in the background. When "Carol of the Bells" came on her eyes felt prickly listening to Rod's favorite.

She didn't mention this because sitting next to Jeff, engaging in getting-to-know-you type conversation, felt almost like a date.

"Are you going to move back sometime?" He said toward the meal's end, breaking a Santa cookie in half.

"I don't have any plans for the future," Janice hedged.

And, a few minutes later, he leaned closer, and whispered, "Would you consider having dinner with me tomorrow night?"

A real date! "That'd be nice," she whispered back.

Before she left, they set a time of 7:30 p.m., and he told her, "I'd like to take you to Henry's—the old Chez Henri's. It's one of my favorites."

Chez Henri! How would it feel to go there with a man other than Rod?

***

The next morning, Janice searched her closet looking for a going-out dress that she didn't associate with Rod. No luck. She called DeeDee and asked for help. Then, she went next door to Ilsa's for words of advice and encouragement.

Ilsa Johnson put a plate of cinnamon rolls in the middle of her round kitchen table. After she heard Janice's concerns, Ilsa said, "Are you feeling disloyal?"

Janice rolled her finger in a circle on the embroidered tablecloth. Holly and red berries felt lumpy to her touch. "I don't think so. It's been a long time." Her throat closed for a couple of seconds. "Rod wouldn't want me to continue mourning the rest of my life."

"You're only forty-five. A lot of time ahead of you." Ilsa filled Janice's coffee cup. "You went to Chez Henri's with him, right?"

"For birthdays and anniversaries...a special place for the two of us." Janice took a small bite of her roll. "We never took Adam and Jesse."

"I went there with my husband." He had died about the time the McKenna's moved in, over twenty years in the past.

After a moment to consider her questions appropriateness, Janice said, "Have you ever dated?"

"That always seemed a lot more effort than it was worth."

Ilsa ran a hand over her new softer, longer hairdo, toned in order to make it shimmer. She'd also lost weight, and her flattering clothes—rich blues and greens and burgundies—set off the silver hair.

When Janice had commented on these changes, Ilsa said, "I'm going to take you up on a visit to the ranch, and wanted to be in better shape when I ride one of those horses of yours."

"And, your hair?" Janice had smirked. "The horses don't care about that."

"Once I slimmed down, other things became important. DeeDee helped me."

"That's no surprise. She's a great consultant. You look fantastic. I can't wait for your visit to Santa Fe." Maybe shopping would be in order. This new Ilsa might like to browse through the many stores and galleries.

"Chez Henri's has been remodeled." Ilsa continued their present conversation. "It won't seem that familiar."

"Familiar or not. It's another thing I need to move on about." Janice pressed her lips together.

"I completely agree." Ilsa patted her hand.

Later that afternoon, DeeDee brought over several outfits that were too small for her. They agreed on a close-fitting, pale gold dress with a slight glow.

"It looks great with your chestnut hair." DeeDee arranged an up-do with tendrils around Janice's face.

Next, she started on Janice's make-up. "Subtle, but enough to bring out those big brown eyes of yours."

As Janice anticipated, DeeDee brought shoes, too. They stuffed the toes with tissues.

"Remember how we used to do this with our bras back in junior high?" DeeDee joked. "At least I did."

"I was too much into horses to care." Janice laughed.

A purse, jewelry, and a bolero jacket in muted shades of gold and rust made Janice look more put together than any time she could remember, even at her own simple, wedding ceremony, held in the hospital administrator's garden and attended by only ten guests. She'd worn a ruffly, ankle-length, green and peach floral dress for the occasion. This ensemble of DeeDee's was a whole lot more sophisticated, and suited her added years.

Standing by a full length mirror, Janice said, "Is this too dressy?"

"It's the Holidays!" DeeDee said.

***

Jeff rang the bell at 7:25 p.m.

When Janice opened the door, his first words were, "Wow! You look terrific."

She merely said, "Thanks." No need to say anything about the assistance garnered.

Glancing around, he said, "This place is homey. It reminds me of where I grew up."

"Most of the furnishings belonged to my mother." Janice scanned the living room, her eyes landing on dark blue velvet-covered pieces and a mahogany credenza that had been placed on a wall of the Montana ranch house's parlor. A gleaming silver coffee and tea service sat on top. When Ilsa dusted and vacuumed the house before Janice arrived, she must have polished the set.

Janice was relieved at how easy it felt to be with Jeff. Easy, yet exciting. As he held her elbow when she sank into the passenger seat of his Audi A4, a tingle like bumping into an electric fencing wire ran through her arm. The inside of the car smelled of new leather, like a bridle fresh out of its packaging.

She never would have recognized Chez Henri. Tables formerly had been arranged in a straight line around the edges of the room. White linen tablecloths had covered those tables, and artfully-folded white linen napkins stood in pointed shapes on top of silver-rimmed dinner plates. At the remodeled Henry's glass-topped tables were placed randomly, and multi-colored napkins were settled into turquoise water goblets. She'd never seen any of the wait staff before, and she learned from information on the large, buff-colored menu that the restaurant was under different ownership.

Chez Henri had specialized in traditional French cuisine with rich sauces. Henry's selections tended toward lighter fare.

After they were seated, Jeff ordered a bottle of Sauvignon Blanc according to Janice's choice.

"I enjoy ones from New Zealand," she had said. These had been Rod's favorites.

"Do you want small plates to share?" Jeff said. "We can try several dishes."

"That sounds terrific. I never know what to get in a restaurant." She couldn't help but think of her usual simple meals at the ranch. "Everything sounds so good."

They started off with a calamari appetizer, followed by a pear and walnut salad, a bowtie pasta dish with crab and capers, roast duck sliders, a cheese and fruit plate for dessert, along with mint chocolate aperitifs.

Best of all was their conversation.

Of course, they talked about marriages, but other things, too.

"We were very happy," Janice said. "Rod's death came without warning. I haven't wanted to date since it happened, so tonight's kind of a...big step."

"Glad it's with me." Yet, Jeff frowned. "You're lucky for the positive memories."

She tilted her head. "How about you?"

"Destined to fail from the start. Can't say there was much positive."

"How sad."

"Children probably would have made a difference. We tried. Susan never wanted to adopt. She was an only child and not used to failure. She couldn't live with it...or with me."

"Where is she?"

"Back in New York. She went to work at her father's financial planning firm."

"Left you here by yourself?"

"By myself." He said it matter-of-factly. "I have plenty to give my life meaning. The kids are great."

Jeff was a pediatrician. "I sing with several groups," he grinned, "including a barbershop quartet."

"That must be fun. I'd like to hear you sometime."

Janice wondered if she should go deeper. She inched into more intimate territory. "I felt deserted when Rod died. Angry and deserted. Everything in my life had some connection to him. Our family, the hospital guild, we jogged together. The Santa Fe ranch has altered my outlook."

"You love it?"

"I do. Especially the horses, and one in particular." Janice told him about Rory.

"I feel the same way about my practice."

Janice pictured him with a calm, reassuring manner, lulling anxious children into a good place. "I'll bet the kids love you."

"My nurse tells me that." He shrugged.

This sparked talk about Janice's own nursing days.

"Didn't you consider going back?"

"Not really. Being cooped up in a hospital wasn't appealing. A need for wide open spaces resurfaced." Luke's weathered face came to mind. "I did take care of the ranch's owner during his last days."

By dessert, she had told Jeff about her mother's early death, and her father's subsequent drinking which caused the loss of their Montana ranch as well as his death. Janice didn't tell Jeff that she'd stayed away, even at that time, letting her brother handle care and details.

Likewise, Jeff had told her about growing up in Minneapolis, the oldest son of an ophthalmologist and his receptionist. His younger brother had joined their father's practice, and he had landed in Seattle for a residency at Children's Hospital.

When he walked Janice to her front door, she paused a moment, wondering about asking him in, but decided next time…

Jeff kissed her on the cheek and walked back to his Audi, a jaunty bounce to his step.

Janice went to sleep in the bed she'd shared with Rod, looking forward to the rest of her visit to Seattle, a smile on her lips.

***

Over the next week, they met twice for festive lunches. On Friday, they went downtown to see the Christmas lights. After dinner at another of Jeff's favorite restaurants, the Northwest Seafood Grill, they stayed in the lounge, listening to soft as butter jazz.

Jeff took her hand when they got out on the street. He sang a few lines of "God Rest Ye Merry Gentlemen" in his comforting voice, and instead of heading for the parking lot, led her down another street by Nordstrom and Macy's. Late-night shoppers bustled by, arms loaded with packages. In the middle of a foot-traffic-only block, a large carousel went round and round, filling the air with tinkling music.

"In case you're too lonesome for Rory, we could go on a ride."

"I haven't been on one of these since I was a kid at the county fair."

"You're never too old."

They rode three times, until both of them were dizzy. Jeff was on a palomino with blue and green trimmings, Janice, alongside him, was on a smaller chestnut decorated in gold.

All the way back to her house, their talk revolved around amusement parks they'd visited. When Janice described trips to Disneyland with her young sons, she spoke of those fun times without a catch in her voice.

Upon arrival at her house, they agreed there had been enough wine earlier in the evening and Jeff joined her in the kitchen to make cocoa.

"My sons will be here tomorrow for our Christmas Eve celebration." Janice sat next to Jeff on the velvet sofa. She'd decided not to introduce him to Adam and Jesse...yet. She did show him photos from an album on the coffee table.

"Next weekend is DeeDee's New Year's party," he said, before leaving. "I'm hoping it'll be special for us."

"Me, too."

His good night kiss tasted like milk chocolate with a hint of peppermint from the candy cane she'd placed in his mug.

That night in bed, she thought about what the next weekend would bring. And, for the first time, she tentatively considered what a move back to Seattle might mean. If that should ever happen, she could put Snake in charge of the ranch. He'd take proper care of it. She could go every few weeks for check-up visits.

At two in the morning, awakening her from a dreamy sleep, the telephone rang. Seconds later, her smile twisted into an expression of anguish.

**

Janice rushed to Rory's stall.

He stood, head hanging low, face stuck in a corner.

"C'mon Boy," she coaxed.

When he didn't respond, she made kissing sounds.

Rory never lifted his head or moved at all.

She entered his stall and crept toward him. She reached out to gently pat his hip. Her hand moved to his barrel. There were no rumbling digestive noises. Janice looked to the other corner at his feedbag. Rory hadn't eaten any of his breakfast. She reached for his shoulder. She scratched behind his ear. Usually he liked this, rubbing his head against her hand.

Rory stayed still.

Is he asleep?

His eyes drooped. He never looked at her.

"It's going to be okay. We'll fix you up." Would they be able to make him better?

Thick liquid dripped from his nostrils as if he had a bad case of the flu.

Janice stroked the velvety, white diamond atop his nose. "I'll be back to check on you soon."

She slipped out and ran for the bunkhouse to find Snake.

The kitchen was dark and empty except for a small Christmas tree, twinkling in the corner.

A minute or two later, Snake switched on the light and entered. "You're here already."

"I took the first flight after you called. How do you think he is?"

"Miserable. Doc Martinez started him on penicillin as soon as his test came back positive."

"Positive for what?"

"Strangles."

"Strangles? What's that?" Is he choking to death?

"The name sounds worse than it is. But, this can be serious, even life-threatening if not treated. His lymph glands are swollen. Hard to swallow."

"That's why he's not eating?"

"Partly. He feels rotten. His temperature has been elevated to about one hundred and five degrees." Snake rubbed the back of his neck.

Janice knew that a horse's normal temperatures ranged from ninety-nine to one hundred and one.

"How long will it last?"

"Hard to say. The other horses have been moved away from him. It's real contagious. So far, none of them have symptoms."

"How'd he get it?"

"Doc says probably at the competitions. Drinking out of communal water troughs. Some infected horse passed it on."

"I received a medical release before taking Rory."

"Somebody must have skipped doing that."

"He should get well, right?" She clasped her hands.

"I hope so."

"He can't even go in the paddocks?"

"Nowhere near the other horses. Dusty's upset, weaving in her new stall, sulking when she's outside." Snake's chest lifted. "You need to use antibacterial spray on everything that comes in contact with him and wash your clothes after being around him and wipe down your boots. Especially the soles."

"Can I groom him? Give him some carrots?"

"You can try. Also, pick his hooves. He'll probably get thrush standing in his stall. Don't feel bad if he refuses the carrots. Think how it is when you're sick."

"I'm going out to him."

"Good idea."

"When I get back, I need to eat." Her head felt woozy. "It was a bumpy flight and I didn't want food."

"I'll cook supper."

Snake had never offered to do this, so Janice wondered what he would make. Worries about Rory quickly pushed this thought aside.

***

After spending half an hour with her unresponsive horse, gently brushing him and talking to him, she went back to the kitchen.

Snake was making omelets. Her own attempts had always turned into a mess. Janice had switched to what she called "Cheese Eggs" which were scrambled, with the omelet filling mixed in. Snake's were perfect, folded over at exactly the right time, golden brown, with green onion, diced tomato and Colby/Jack cheese in the middle. He heated Canadian Bacon and served it on the side, along with applesauce, whole wheat toast and marmalade.

"Breakfast for supper," he said.

"Comfort food," she responded.

They ate in silence for a few minutes, until Snake said, "You doing all right?"

"I guess not." Janice sniffed and wiped her eyes with a tissue.

"This is hard."

"That's for sure." Should I go on? "When I first came here...I felt broken. I didn't know if I'd ever mend."

"That's natural given your situation."

"Rod had been gone less than a year. I wasn't adjusting."

"Understandable."

"I was hopeful about the change of scenery, being in a place I didn't associate with him."

"I can see that."

"This ranch gave me something to focus on, and Rory has been a huge part of that. Some winter mornings, I've had to force myself out of bed. I'd wander out to see him, and soon I hurried with my chores so we could go for a ride. There's something about a horse, a special horse, one you connect with...it's hard to explain."

"You're doing fine."

"I had that kind of horse as a girl. When I lost my mother, being with Tinker was the only thing that made me forget my grief. When I was with him, every sad thought, every tear left me. It's been the same with Rory. When Luke died it brought back all my other losses. I'd rub Rory's shoulder, and it was like he absorbed the hurt. Now, he's sick and won't even look at me."

Janice brushed her cheek and dropped her head into crossed arms.

Snake pulled his chair next to her and carefully stroked her hair.

"I'm sorry." She squeezed her eyes tightly shut. "I hate to be such a baby."

"You're not. It's okay to feel bad. It's okay to worry about him."

"Thanks, Snake...for the meal, for listening...for being my friend." Her voice was muffled.

"That's what I'm here for."

"And Snake..."

"Yeah?"

She lifted her head. "What's your real name?"

After a hesitation, he stammered, "Wilbur...I don't tell many people."

"Can I call you Will?"

"Sure. When we're alone."

***

The next day, Janice called DeeDee.

"I was shocked when you left so hurriedly." She sounded even more intense than usual. "Why didn't you tell me? I had to check with Ilsa when you didn't answer your phone."

"My horse is sick and I needed to come right home to him."

"Your horse? You needed to go home?"

Janice listened to DeeDee's heavy breathing.

"I don't get it. What about Adam and Jesse?"

"Both are happy to stay in Bellingham with their girlfriends."

"I thought you'd be moving back, especially once you got to know Jeff. That's not going to happen, is it?"

This is where I belong. I was blinded by the Christmas lights. "I'll come to Seattle for visits, but I'm staying here."

39

"Jeff will be disappointed."

"I wrote him a note. He's a great guy with a lot to offer. He's going to find someone."

"He will...Actually, there is a nurse in his office."

"I'm glad."

Jeff never contacted Janice.

***

Twice a week Doctor Martinez came to the ranch and did nose swabs. The Strangles epidemic lasted three months, with one horse after another succumbing to elevated temperatures, flu-like symptoms, and positive tests. Of fifteen horses, the only one not to get sick was Dusty, even though she tested positive, too.

The vet finally said, "I want to scope her. See what's going on."

Janice watched as he stuck a tube into Dusty's nostrils and examined the airways.

"She's your carrier. Dusty brought the infection to your place."

"Why hasn't she gotten sick?" Janice rubbed Dusty's neck.

"She picked it up in the past and the bacteria never left her. Carriers spread the illness to other horses."

"Did Palmer know this when he gave her to Janice?" Snake, in an uncharacteristic way, interrupted.

"Hard to say." Doctor Martinez shrugged.

"Have you been called to his place for Strangles?" Snake pressed.

"You need to talk to him."

With three consecutive negative tests at weekly intervals, Rory was at last cleared by the vet. As important to Janice, Rory seemed like his old self. Later that day, she planned to take him for an easy trail ride, expecting he might be frisky from the long isolation.

Doctor Martinez also sedated Dusty, and started the process of removing inflammatory material.

After he drove off in his white van, Snake said, "We need to go talk to Fred Palmer."

"Right now?"

"Right now."

Janice gave Rory a couple of carrots, and told him, "I'll be back in a little while and we'll go for our ride."

Upon arriving at Palmer's place, Janice and Snake found him mucking out a stall, and complaining loudly. "Damn that idiot woman. Never should've hired her."

"Excuse me, Fred, could we have a word with you?" Snake stood away from a wheelbarrow as Palmer hurled dirty bedding into it.

Janice stood next to Snake.

"Didn't hear you come up. I got four more stalls to clean before dinner."

"Where's Angie?" Janice asked.

"Fired her."

"How come?" It was unusual for Snake to delve into someone's personal business like this.

"She's a thief. That's why. Caught her taking twenties from my cash box."

"Where did she go?"

"Hanging out at the casino, I expect. Maybe she got a job there."

"Could she have gone back to Pittsburgh?"

"I don't know and I don't care. Can't have a thief around here." Palmer leaned on his pitchfork. "What do you want to talk to me about?"

"It's Dusty, Fred," Janice started.

"What about her?" Palmer tucked his chin and narrowed his eyes.

"I don't know if you heard. We've had an epidemic of Strangles at my place."

"I got wind of it."

"Doctor Martinez told us Dusty was the carrier."

"Sorry about that."

"Did you have any idea of this when you gave her to Janice?" Snake's mouth hardened into a straight line.

"None whatsoever."

"Have your horses been sick?"

43

"No they have not! What are you getting at, Snake?"

"Merely asking."

"My horses are healthy."

"We wanted to check."

"You got all I know." Palmer turned away dismissively, digging his pitchfork into the bedding.

As Snake drove away from Palmer's small spread, Janice said, "He was awfully mad."

"Defensive if you ask me. He could be lying." Snake rapped a hand on the steering wheel.

"Why?"

"He approached Luke around the time of the final illness. Wanted to buy Cerrillos. Luke told him he'd willed it to you. It's common knowledge that Palmer would like to expand."

"Looks as if he has more than enough to take care of with Angie gone."

"That's another story." Snake shrugged. "Palmer could have known Dusty was a carrier and sent her over to infect your horses, thinking this kind of problem would make you more than willing to sell."

"He didn't know you were helping out?"

"I guess not."

"This is all speculation, right? We'll probably never find out if it was intentional on his part."

"Probably not."

"We do know I'm staying." Janice stuck out her round chin. Then, she considered saying something else that had been on her mind since before the Seattle trip. "And, I think we should talk about you taking a bigger role. Who knows, maybe we could do some expanding. Luke used to run a pack service taking riders into the wilderness, before he downsized to short trail rides. You'd make a good partner, Will."

"I appreciate your confidence."

"What about Angie? Did that come as a surprise?"

"Not a bit. I'm free to say...it's what happened to me. I took her in temporarily after she showed up after her husband, my old friend with the Pittsburgh police force, kicked her out. Big mistake. She only stayed a week, but in that time stole all my cash.

She's a gambler, and doesn't have any scruples about getting money wherever she can."

"That's awful."

"She needs help. I'm hoping she went back to Pittsburgh to get it. No matter, I'm betting we don't see her again."

"I hope that's the case."

"Let's stop for dinner in town...on me."

"Why Will, that's a great idea. I haven't been out to a restaurant in Santa Fe for a good long while."

"If there was someone to watch over the horses, we could catch a movie."

"Maybe there's something on television."

"Sounds good." His expression turned un-expectedly timid. "And hey, you can call me Will anytime...around anyone. I kind of like it."

***

By the time they got back from an enchilada dinner at Lucy's Casita, early evening had set in. Still, there would be enough light for Janice to go with Rory on a short walk.

She saddled him up and headed to the top of Luke's mesa. Their ride was easy and smooth. He wasn't the least bit riled up, seeming calm to be with her in this way.

Once there, she hopped off and stood watching the sky change from pink to orange to dark purple, and was reminded of another sunset when first deciding to stay at Cerrillos.

She'd stood in a hotel window with her friend DeeDee, and felt an eagerness for the new direction her life might be taking.

Now, up on the mesa, looking down at the ranch, she sensed Luke's presence. "I thought about staying in Seattle. I'm so sorry. I almost forgot my promise to you."

It was as if he put an understanding hand on her shoulder.

Holding the reins slack in one hand, she rubbed Rory's neck with the other.

"And, how could I ever consider leaving you?" She traced the white "R" on his forehead with her fingertip, and then lightly kissed the diamond atop his nose.

Rory stretched, gave a long sighing breath, and moved closer to Janice.

"We're going to make some changes around our place. More horses, who knows what else. And, Will is going to be a big part of this. Who knows what that's going to mean..."

The sky gradually darkened, and stars began to pop out. Janice watched their twinkling and gave another thought to Luke and his long-lost daughter, before re-mounting Rory.

She whispered, "Time to go, Boy, while we can still see the trail all the way back home."

Kathleen and Stanley at
Archway Equestrian Sports

AUTHOR'S BIOGRAPHY

Kathleen Glassburn earned an MFA in Creative Writing from Antioch University, Los Angeles. Currently, she resides in Edmonds, Washington with her husband, three dogs, two cats, and a 45-year-old turtle. When not writing or reading, she likes to play the piano and horseback ride. Her work has been published or is forthcoming in *Amarillo Bay*, *Blue Lake Review*, *Cactus Heart Press*, *Cadillac Cicatrix*, *Cairn*, *Crucible*, *Epiphany Magazine*, *Imitation Fruit*, *Lullwater Review*, *Marco Polo Quarterly*, *Rio Grande Review*, *RiverSedge*, *SLAB*, *The Talon Mag*, *Wild Violet*, *The Writer's Workshop Review* and several other journals. Her story, "Picnics," was a finalist in *Glimmer Train's* Best Start contest. She is Managing Editor of The Writer's Workshop Review (www.thewritersworkshopreview.net).

For further information, please see her website: www.kathleenglassburn.com

THE DIME NOVEL IS MAKING A COMEBACK!

Originating in the late 19th-century and seeing its heyday in the 1940s and 1950s, particularly in genres such as the Western, the format became an important influence on the comic book, the radio drama, and the film and television treatment. Today's "flash novel" is really a new take on an old idea: stories just shy of novelette length, with single to numbered chapters rather than asterisks, and which, like the movies, compress a narrative otherwise "novelistic" in scope into a short form suitable for a single reading or download.

Red Dashboard LLC is a small indie publishing house seeking intriguing books of poetry and literature: poetry (chapbook and full-length), flash and short story collections, non-fiction, black-and-white artwork.

THE DESERT DIME NOVEL TRILOGY

by M.V. Montgomery

BOOK 1

Mark Twain in Outer Space is a comic space western featuring a not-so-innocent abroad. It also offers a serious reflection upon the universality of storytelling, and the dangers of getting carried away with the sound of one's own words.

BOOK 2

The Double Dare Devil features Skip Eubanks, an old cowboy-turned-stuntman who is paralyzed after a fall from a helicopter. His wife Bonnie now runs the business, but something very sinister is happening to the stuntmen she supplies to the studios.

BOOK 3

Trouble in Paradise Valley tells the story of a big budget Hollywood production that somehow survives star egos, several rewrites, and its own faulty premise. But how long can it last when it intrudes onto a site once sacred to Hohokam skywatchers

OTHER DIME NOVEL SERIES

Ghost Cow Trail
By Doc Hudson

The Maiden-head Mask
By Bill Plank

Sunset "Gold" Canyon
Fire on the Brazos
Forthcoming, 2015—Bekke's Law
By J.W. Edwards

Mall of the Damned
By Tyson West

Creating Florinda
Creando a Florinda- Spanish
By Anita Haas

Radio Tales
By Matthew Kirshman

The Santa Fe Trilogy I—A New Plateau
& Ridin' High
By Kathleen Glassburn

The Bottle Opener
By Laura Madeline Wiseman

www.reddashboard.com

Made in the USA
Lexington, KY
21 September 2017